Robert Armstrong

Chimneys for Furnaces, Fire-Places, and Steam Boilers

Robert Armstrong

Chimneys for Furnaces, Fire-Places, and Steam Boilers

ISBN/EAN: 9783337256777

Printed in Europe, USA, Canada, Australia, Japan

Cover: Foto ©Andreas Hilbeck / pixelio.de

More available books at **www.hansebooks.com**

CHIMNEYS

— FOR —

FURNACES, FIRE-PLACES,

— AND —

STEAM BOILERS.

By R. ARMSTRONG, C. E.

SECOND AMERICAN EDITION.

TO WHICH IS APPENDED AN ESSAY ON

HIGH CHIMNEYS.

By PROF. L. PINZGER,

Of L'Ecole Polytechnique at Aix-la-Chappelle.

NEW YORK:

D. VAN NOSTRAND, PUBLISHER,

23 MURRAY AND 27 WARREN STREET.

1883.

CHIMNEYS FOR FURNACES

FIRE-PLACES,

AND

STEAM BOILERS.

———• • •———

PRACTICAL THERMODYNAMICS.

FURNACES, or closed fire-places, which it is the main design of this essay to treat upon, are essentially different in principle and construction to the ordinary open fire-places of dwelling-houses, as they are exceedingly different in the general scope and object, and in the vast variety of their applications; yet there is one thing common and important to both, and that is the chimney, or vertical flue, for the purpose of creating a proper draught of air through the fire, as well as to carry off the smoke, or other products of combustion; and it is in the generally in-

creased proportions of this almost in-
dispensable adjunct to all furnaces which
principally distinguishes the modern from
the ancient practice of steam engineering.

The great development of the manufacturing system of this country during
the last twenty or thirty years, and the
erection of a larger description of factories
being required, has caused more attention to be devoted to the stability and
general economy of such structures, in
which the erection of larger chimneys
than formerly have in some degree par-
ticipated, but only to a trifling extent
from professional architects, properly so
called. The external portions of the
chimneys of dwelling-houses have, no
doubt, had some share of attention from
architects, but it may be doubted
whether the most important function of
even a house chimney—the creation of
draught—has been adequately considered,
even if only to prevent that greatest of
all nuisances, a smoky house. In proof
of which, many cases might be cited

among the mansions of the nobility and
gentry all over the country, as well as in
town, where it is less excusable. Indeed,
the chimney flues of dwelling-houses are
too commonly treated as mere conduits
for smoke, as, in fact, they are frequently
termed, and as such they are considered
equally subordinate with drains and
other conduits, which may or may not be
attended to after the plan of the house is
determined upon, and, in some cases,
even after the house is partly erected,
instead of being—as I humbly think they
ought to be—considered, in an architectural sense at least, of the highest importance, as they are, in fact, the highest
external features that can in this climate
properly characterize the well-ventilated,
well-warmed, healthy, and comfortable
dwellings of a rational and civilized com-
munity.

It is far from my intention to write a
homily on any branch of architecture as
an art, but it must be admitted that there
are few, if any, subjects of such useful
importance connected with architecture

that have been so much neglected, misdirected, and misunderstood, as the proper construction of chimneys generally, or their proportions most suitable to the various purposes for which they are designed. Such attention as house chimneys have hitherto received, has been too commonly in respect of their ornamental and decorative character only, even to the extent of erecting fictitious chimneys where there are no flues and none wanted. For all purposes of real utility the house-building architect too often, apparently, contents himself with a single step, and in some respects scarcely so much, in advance of the "hole in the wall" of the ancient Romans, who, however, with all their barbarous simplicity, were, at any rate, never troubled with down draughts —the universal malady of all English smoky dwelling-houses.

The labored ornamentation of house-tops, with their numerous little crooked outlets for smoke, though frequently only inlets for wind and rain, mis-termed chimneys, have been the chief degradation of modern architectural science. The art of erecting chimneys for steam-engines, and for similar purposes, has, however, fared somewhat better, since all the more substantially useful part of architecture, comprising nearly the whole of that appertaining to manufacturing industry, has for some time past, in our northern counties at least, merged into the province of the civil and mechanical engineer, technically known in Lancashire as the factory engineer.

Factory engineers, however, though differing widely from architects generally on many points, are not at all agreed among themselves as to the best form and construction of a chimney for attaining the principal end in view; namely, the best draught at the least expense. In short, the problem of how to give a sufficient velocity to the air passing through the fire-grate, with a given temperature in the furnace or in the escaping products, and at a minimum rate of consumption of the fuel to be used, has scarcely yet received and adequate solution, even theoretically. Practically, the question has received many solutions—too many, one may say, for the convenience of ordinary business men—which circumstance is one of the main causes that has rendered the present work necessary, as well as contributing to some of its chief difficulties. The multitude and diversity of opinions on this subject may, in a great measure, be ascribed to the generally prevailing reliance on the dicta of some few popular professors, or rather amateurs, of chemistry; in which category we might also, perhaps without much injustice, include a few so-called scientific guide-books. I am not for decrying the present inundation of cheap scientific treatises, which is so marked a feature of the times; but, on the contrary, think such books cannot be too many nor too cheap, when original or genuine. Such of them, however, as are merely reproductions of the last century, or even the early part of the present, are generally to be deprecated.

To make a chemical laboratory, for instance, as has sometimes been done, an object of study to the engineer or builder, however scientifically constructed and arranged, unless, indeed, the object be to erect another laboratory for a similar purpose, is, to say the least, very injudicious, and the fruitful source of much error and prejudice in the minds of young men of scientific aspirations. More particularly is this the case when the object in view is the arrangement of factories or works for other special purposes; those purposes being mainly for commercial profit, and not for the mere amusement of amateurs, nor even for the professed advancement of science, which is often little better.

Holding the above views in common with the factory engineers before adverted to, I have always preferred taking for precedents the blacksmith's forge, the potter's kiln, or the glasshouse chimney, rather than seek mechanical prescriptions, so to speak, among the crucibles and alembics of our " modern alchemists."

With respect to the fire-place itself— the Furnace—to which a chimney of some kind is but a necessary though highly important accessory, it is altogether in a different predicament. The chief peculiarity relating to Furnaces, is that they have always been, and are necessarily, in the hands, or constantly under the immediate control, of the workman himself. To him they are, in a certain sense, his tools—the tools of his trade—and for each special trade comparatively perfect, at least he thinks so. Operative workmen, at any rate, though "reformers" they may be themselves, seldom willingly admit of any reform in their work tools. On this point they are essentially conservative in all trades, even to the cobler, as he sings, "To loose my awl 't would break my heart," etc. The consequence of this general feeling is that we have an abundance of experiments confirmatory, or otherwise, of any particular innovations or alterations in a chimney or furnace that effect the draught, which is the only result a workman cares about. If the alteration turns out an improvement, it is quickly, and almost instinctively, as it were, appreciated; if the reverse, or doubtful, or if even only undecided, it is as quickly rejected and condemned. Generally rather too quickly, in fact, for the interest of such inventors and improvers as cannot afford to wait for matured results. Hence has arisen a good deal of that great diversity of opinion, not to say theory, even among the most observant of mechanical engineers themselves.

The Chimney and Furnace have not been sufficiently considered together, or as one apparatus. The Forge furnace, the Steam Boiler furnace, the Baker's Oven furnace, and the Brick-kiln furnace, may be instanced as four examples of great dissimilarity of purpose; but from the first to the fourth consecutively, requiring a gradually decreasing velocity of draught. The first and the last of the series, being instances of the two opposite extremes, requiring the quickest and the slowest draughts, and having in consequence the highest and the lowest temperatures. These two extreme cases, moreover, have one peculiarity in common, which is, that it is by many considered a difficult matter to decide in either case where the furnace proper ends, and where the chimney flue begins. Although I shall have to revert to this point more fully in the sequel, it may here be observed that the difficulty alluded to may be greatly lessened by considering that the termination or vent of the Forge or Air furnace for working iron ought to be at no great distance beyond the point of greatest temperature of the flame, because, in the Forge, or Iron furnace especially, it is the flame that "does the work." Whereas in the other extreme case mentioned—the Brick-kiln—which requires little or no flame, the furnace may be considered to terminate at the lowest possible temperature of the issuing hot air, and might in fact do very well with hardly any chimney at all. The other two kinds of furnaces referred to—the Steam-engine furnace and the

Baker's Oven furnace—may be considered
generally in an intermediate condition to
the above, or in the order in which they
are stated, more particularly as respects
strength and draught. These two furnaces have also one trait in common, in
so far as they both require regulating
while at work, and are capable of permit-
ting of variations of temperature through
a very considerable range. The steam
boiler furnace admits of great delicacy as
well—so much so, as to make it, when
supplied with proper self-acting dampers,
a very efficient regulator or governor to
the steam-engine itself. In the Oven
furnace, the draught requires to be
" sharpened" or slackened, from time to
time, by hand, to suit the kind of goods
undergoing the operation of baking.
The steam-engine furnace is like the
forge furnace, so far as it requires occasionally a very quick action for raising
the pressure of steam in a short time, or
otherwise, to prevent the steam from going down by some sudden increase of
the load on the engine. The Oven fur-

nace is not subject to such sudden
changes, but rather requires a long-con-
tinued, persistent, steady heat. This
property of the Oven furnace is mainly
caused by the large mass of brickwork
with which it is commonly constructed,
absorbing and retaining a great deal of
heat to begin with.

The accumulation and retention of
heat, or of the power of heating other
bodies, by non-conducting or slow-con-
ducting substances used in the construction of some furnaces, and the rapid dis-
sipation and apparent extinction of the
same, by metallic or good conducting
substances, in connection with other furnaces so provided, is perhaps the most
interesting branch of this subject, and as
anything bearing on this that may serve
to elucidate the principles on which
sound practice, to say nothing of theory,
must be sooner or later established, this
introductory Essay appears to be the
proper place in which to introduce what
is either new, or differently treated and
usual.

In following the course here indicated,
I am quite aware of the unmethodical appearance it must have : but I have always preferred the rough and useful,
though only prospectively recompensed
labors of the pioneer's track, to the
smooth greensward and well-worn walks
of science that often lead " to nowhere."
Satisfied if, in going through the still un-
explored fields of discovery, I can bring
home but a few rough logs towards the
building up of the edifice so recently
founded for sheltering the yet young
though promising science of Heat and
its relations, now termed Thermo-dy-
namics.

For the actual state and condition of
much of existing knowledge on the subject of heat, there is now no longer occasion to go for comparisons back to the
times of Bacon, Newton, and Hooke,
much as is due to those illustrious phil-
osophers. Nor is there any occasion to
consult the works of Franklin, Black,
Rumford, ond others of their times, nor
adopt any of the theories and doctrines

they promulgated. The opinions of those much more reliable authorities—even Young, Dalton, and Davy—cannot now be taken without some little reserve; but the experiments of their distinguished successors Faraday and Joule, with the praiseworthy labors of Rankine, Tindal, and a few others in the same direction, have more recently furnished results on the subject of the present inquiry which cannot be too highly esteemed, and which with this general acknowledgment, I intend to make a free use of in the course of this work.

There is no need to extend the present Essay by any long dissertation on the theory of Chimney draught, neither shall I introduce much of what has been advanced by others on that subject, but rather confine these remarks to such elementary facts, principles, and rules as are likely to be useful to those practical engineers, builders and others, whose commercial undertakings—contracts and other exigencies—do not generally admit of long delay, much study, or scien_ tific research, but who, nevertheless, may wish to readily avail themselves of a few leading principles and practical directions, such as may at least prevent them from getting very far wrong. By propounding and exemplifying a series of practical examples of cases that can be now referred to in actual use, it is hoped that the most casual reader will be able to accompany me with confidence and satisfaction through the rest of these Essays.

THE STEAM-HEATING CHIMNEY.

The questions of most interest in connection with large chimneys, and those usually the first asked, after the important one of cost, by the capitalist who has determined on some considerable outlay, either in erecting a new shaft or rebuilding an old one, may be classed under two principal heads—namely, the external and the internal proportions.

Whether the external form of a hollow shaft of brickwork or masonry of considerable elevation, in this climate and country, should be a plain obelisk, or a finely proportioned architectural column, is a question that does not admit of much difficulty in deciding. Most engineers are no doubt properly inclined to the opinion that for so entirely utilitarian a purpose as a chimney, the former is the most preferable. It is, however, quite a matter of architectural taste as to how it may harmonize with surrounding objects, and the last thing in the world, perhaps, that engineers ought to dogmatize upon. Whether the form of such a column should affect great simplicity—a simple truncated cone or pyramid, for instance, decreasing uniformly in diameter upwards ; or whether it should affect great stability, like the trunk of the oak, proverbially the shape for withstanding a severe gale of wind ; or, ought a chimney shaft to be erected with a variable batter, like a lighthouse or a monument on the sea-coast—these are all questions requiring some consideration in designing a chimney for general purposes ; but for the chimney of a steam-engine other

especial requirements of **far greater im-**
portance are to be considered.

It is the internal proportions of a chimney shaft only—its height and sectional
area—that principally concern the steam
engineer. Until these essential internal
proportions are first agreed upon, we are
not in a position to discuss the external
proportions with advantage.

In fixing on the proper dimensions of
the vertical smoke flue, or inside of a
steam-engine chimney, it is a question
with many whether it should, as is most
commonly done, be tapered internally or
diminished in area towards the top; or
whether it ought to be parallel—as wide
at top as at bottom—in order to have the
greatest velocity of draught. Or, again,
ought a chimney to be, as some few ec-
centric engineers contend, and occasionally carry into execution, even wider at
the top than the bottom?

These questions are all deserving of
attentive consideration, and will receive
ample illustration in the sequel. But
there is another question quite as impor-

tant as any of the above, and requiring a
prior consideration. It is thus enunci-
ated: What are the proper dimensions—
height and area—of a chimney shaft most
suitable for a steam-engine of any given
number of horse-power, or, which is
nearly the same thing, for burning away
a given quantity of coals per hour? The
proper answer to this question depends a
good deal on the quality of the coals
used and the quantity of waste gaseous products arising from their generally
imperfect combustion in the furnace.
The best Newcastle or Hartley coals, and
the best Welsh steam coal, though requiring very different treatment in the
furnace, are found equally in practice not
to require such large chimneys as the inferior coals of the midland and manufacturing districts of England. Under these
circumstances it will perhaps be most ad-
visable, in the first instance, to base our
observations and calculations on such
practical data as those districts so readily
afford, more particularly those of Lancashire, South Yorkshire, Derbyshire, and

Staffordshire. Another reason for adopting those data is, that the usual stoking and management of the fires in those districts may be described as a fair medium between the north and the south, between the Newcastle and the Cornish practice. There is one feature in common between the northern and southern practice that may be mentioned, which is, that the engines in both districts are generally very lightly loaded, compared with those in the manufacturing districts; the latter being very seldom, indeed, working at less than 50 per cent. above their nominal horse-power, and commonly more than double their real or indicated horse-power.

The last-mentioned circumstance furnishes us with the reason for the maxim so long prevalent in Lancashire, that a steam-engine chimney, leaving all considerations of cost out of the question, can never be too large nor too powerful, provided it is supplied with efficient means for checking the draught, by properly fitted dampers or otherwise, whereby the supply of steam can be readily controlled at any moment, so as to work the engine at one-half its full·power, and using considerably less than one-half the power of draught of the chimney; for which purpose the ordinary damper (say 3 ft. long) of a thirty-horse engine ought to be open only to the extent of 3 to 6 in., thus having a surplus draught always at command for emergencies.

Another feature of this question arising from the practice of working steam-engines with inferior fuel, is the large proportion of dirt and small ashes derived from the burning of the bad coal—the " flue-dust "—which accumulates to an enormous extent within the flues and on the bottom of the chimney. Much of this fine dust—all the finer particles especially, and to a much greater extent than has hitherto been suspected, or at least recognized—passes up and out of the chimney top under the appearance of smoke, but which even veteran "smoke burners " generally are surprised to find is neither carbonaceous soot nor combustible **gas,** but principally incombustible earthy and **silicious** dust.

In appealing to **the** practice of our best engineers respecting the proper area of the vertical chimney flue of a steam-engine, there is no occasion to go back to the times of Brindley and Smeaton—when steam-engines were called fire-engines, and the firemen first called stokers excepting for the purpose of making a single reference to the early practice of the celebrated James Watt, which strikingly illustrates, not only the difficulty of determining *a priori* the right proportions of a chimney, but also the admirable caution and prudence observed by him in this, as in other matters, so remarkably conspicuous in the eminently practical mind of that great man.

After Mr. Watt had once ascertained the best size and proportions of a chimney most suitable for a given size of boiler and engine, he did not at first, as almost any tyro of the present day would not hesitate to do—venture to throw the draught of two such or similar boilers

into one chimney of a larger area, so that
the same outlet might serve for the
smoke from both furnaces, but he actu-
ally erected two such chimneys alongside
each other! Or, occasionally, he did
what was equivalent thereto: in erecting
a chimney for two boilers, he would
build up a midfeather, or division wall,
from bottom to top, in order to separate
the two draught currents from each
other, in the same manner as in house
chimneys. Had we not the evidence of
yet existing erections to the fact, such a
statement at this distance of time might
be considered scarcely credible.*

From all accounts of Mr. Watt's early
practice, it may be fairly inferred that he
did not theorize much respecting the

---

* Two united chimneys of this kind were, not many
years ago, in use, with two of Boulton and Watt's
original 20-horse boilers, in the cotton-spinning works
of Messrs. John Pooley & Sons, in Manchester. The
case was remarkable, from the fact that the engineer
of the firm once attempted to improve (as he thought)
the draught of the chimney by breaking an opening
through the midfeather, in order that the smoke
might fill both flues. The result was, the draught was
entirely lost, and the communication had to be closed
up again before the engine could be got to work.

height of engine chimneys; for, having succeeded in doubling the effect of the steam-engine itself, for the same amount of fuel previously used, he found no difficulty in making a low chimney suffice, such, in fact, as were then in use for the old atmospheric engines, and occasionally to be seen in the mining districts at the present time. Those primitive erections, however—mere outlets for smoke—can now hardly be considered as chimneys at all, seldom exceeding an elevation of two or three yards higher than the top of the boiler. So soon, however, as the double-powered steam-engine came into use, which quadrupled in effect the "old atmospheric," and often exceeded that, when applied to turning machinery in towns, it was found that the speed of the engine was often reduced for want of steam, and that again for want of sufficient draught. This last was occasioned, not unfrequently, strange as the words may now sound in the ears of modern engine-drivers, by an "unfavorable wind!"

Prior to the times we are speaking of

the height of an engine chimney shaft, or
stack of chimneys, as on Mr. Watt's system the chimney was, in fact, did not
then appear to be of much consequence,
provided it exceeded that of the neigh-
boring buildings, and any precedents
that then existed for the area of the aperture or exit passage of the smoke were
like those for the height—of a very anti-
quated and empirical character. The
size and shape of the superior orifice of
a chimney was, in fact, even within the
present century, regulated by no fixed
rule, but was variously modified, as well
also in diameter and area, from accident-
al circumstances—often by considerations
as to what could be made safely to stand,
should the chimney require raising a
little higher than usual, or than first intended. The numerous envious rivals of
Boulton and Watt in the early part of the
present century, the Sheratts, Murrays,
and others of that time, whose almost
universal rule was to give "one inch
more in diameter of cylinder than Watt"
for the same nominal horse-power, "and

for a great deal less money," had no little share in helping to mend this state of things. They all knew pretty well how important it was to have a little extra steam, to meet the possible imperfect performances of their engines, and this a very few inches or feet of extra brickwork in the width and height of the chimney always gave them the command of, though this was often done at the casual suggestion of the bricklayer. In this matter, as with a corresponding suggestion of raising the height of the feed-pipes, which was often complied with professedly to suit the convenience of the stoker in preventing boilng over, it generally resulted in raising the pressure of the steam—an infallible remedy for almost all other deficiencies. Thus it occasionally happened that the trifling or crude suggestion of the bricklayer or stoker, in some instances, turned favorably the tide of success, which first founded the establishment of some of the largest engineering firms.

It is owing to similar circumstances to

those just referred to that we have so many examples of engine and other chimneys in most of our old provincial towns, which, on being raised higher than at first intended, have been stayed from time to time by means of iron tie-rods, and hooped with iron bands. These iron rods, props and crutches to chimneys are much resorted to in breweries, distilleries, malt kilns, and other large works, as well in London as in different parts of the south of England, and are very far from being any indication of want of great prosperity in the commercial and manufacturing concerns to which they are attached. In their apparent condition they are the very opposite to the establishments of even second-rate manufacturers in Lancashire.

So far as economy of fuel is concerned, the great prosperity and wealth of the former seems to be in defiance of extravagant waste and temporary expedients; while in the latter it arises in a great measure from well-considered permanent arrangements in all that concerns their engines, boilers and furnaces. The necessity of artificial helps to **the** stability **of a chimney** is a sure manifestation of **great waste of** fuel, by unnecessary stoking **and forcing the fires, and** thereby **overheating the chimneys through** inadequate **area of flue.** On the other hand, **we** may instance the **air furnaces and** kilns of the iron works and potteries of Staffordshire, **where there is some** degree **of** necessity **for resorting to the** expedients referred to, **on account of the** much higher temperature **required by the** process going **on within the furnace.**

The chimneys, **or conè, of an iron furnace,** an earthenware **kiln, or a** glasshouse, **is, in fact, a part of the furnace itself, or at least ought to be so considered, and necessarily becomes heated by the** flame **passing into, through, or among the materials and articles of manufacture it contains. This peculiarity,** which is **also common to many varieties of** chemical **furnaces as well as to pottery kilns, is the main cause of the very strong** draught therein obtained.

In the case of a steam engine boiler furnace, however, it is well known that no such thing as the flame passing off into the chimney, nor even into a flue leading thereto, after leaving the bottom or internal tube of the boiler, is admissible with the slightest attention to economy of fuel. It requires but little consideration to convince us that the flame of a steam-engine furnace ought to be wholly expended against the boiler bottom, or, where internal furnaces or flues are used, entirely within the boiler itself, in which case the draught is created solely by the ascensional force of the column of waste air or smoke within the chimney, heated to the comparatively moderate temperature of 500 or 600 deg.

Thus it will be observed, there is a wide distinction to be made between these two species of furnaces; the steam-engine furnace approaching more nearly, in its moderate temperature, economy, and other circumstances, to the enclosed house stove, or at least to the kitchen fire-place, or cooking range. In these, the grate-room or furnace proper, and the chimney or smoke flue, are essentially separate and distinct parts, though in the best construction of engine furnaces they are rendered more perfectly so by interposing what has been always considered and properly termed the flame chamber, or flame bed,* by practical engineers.

On the other hand, in the action of the air furnaces of a potter's kiln, in which the vertical flame chamber and chimney are both in one, or in the small furnaces of a chemist's laboratory, arranged for producing very perfect combustion and the most intense heats only, of two or three thousand degrees and upwards, we find a very different state of things to that of a steam boiler, requiring a heat only a little beyond that of boiling water.

* Several other more or less affected terms are applied to this part of a furnace by the ultra-chemical school of smoke prevention patentees; such as mixing chamber and diffusing chamber, of which the term combustion chamber is perhaps the least inappropriate, although, in reality, combustion goes on more vigorously in the grate-room than anywhere else.

The importance of the distinctions we have thus endeavored—though perhaps imperfectly—to point out, though well understoed by practical firemen, has been much underrated, and the cause of some dogmatism and misapprehension, especially on the smoke question. From this mixing up of different species of furnaces, intended for totally different objects and processes of art, though each may be practically perfect for the purpose it is intended for, very iucorrect conclusions only have been deduced by some scientific writers. Waiving, therefore, for the present any further consideration in this place of the variable opinions of those chemists who have not yet been able to define satisfactorily where the steam-engine or other furnace (proper) ends, or where the chimney flue begins,—and dismissing also the calculations of those really able mathematicians on the subject of the velocity of draught, whose conclusions on the question have, unfortunately, differed from each other by nearly 500 per cent. we shall next proceed to de-

scribe the design for a steam engine
chimney, hastily improvised for a partic-
clar occasion, and which, on being properly executed, happened to be right. We
use this expression purposely, not wish-
ing to claim any particular merit for the
design itself, and do not say how many
others we may have taken more pains
with, that, from various causes, have
turned out less successful, although as in-
structive lessons, some such may be referred to in the sequel.

In order to elucidate the object of this
chapter still further, and to show what
confused and erroneous notions on the
subject of draught in chimneys have
been, from time to time, prevalent, even
in so generally intelligent and eminently
manufacturing a town as Manchester, the
following extract from a letter addressed
to one of the newspapers in that city is
inserted, together with my reply thereto.
The article was entitled "Smoke and Long
Chimneys," and commenced as follows:

"The writer proposes that, instead of
erecting a long chimney for a steam-en-

gine furnace, a very long and wide flue or chamber should be built, contiguous to the furnace. Take an area of ten yards by twenty, more or less, according to the size of the furnace, wall it round 10 ft. high, and build three or four crosswalls, 3 ft. short of the length of the chamber, each alternately, the alternate end of each wall being tied into the outer walls, arching the whole over from wall to wall, or covering it with flags (any more convenient form might be adopted, provided the length and height of the flue was obtained)—the smoke and rarefied air from the furnace to be conveyed by an ordiary-sized flue into it at one corner, passing through it zig-zag to the end, and then up the chimney, which need not be higher than the buildings around. There should be a door into it, at some convenient place, to take out the soot; and at the first time it was started it would be necessary to put in a quantity of shavings and light them, in order to start the draught; this would only be required when it was first commenced with, or after it had been a long time out of use.

"The writer conceives that, when the flue is filled with the smoke and rarefied air from the furnace, there would be a partial—and but a partial—vacuum in the flue, or that the volume of air in it would not be of equal density with the surrounding atmosphere, and that the difference in the specific gravity of the smoke and hot air in the whole flue, and the like quantity of atmosphere, would be so great that the air would rush through the furnace with great force to effect an equilibrium, thereby creating an intense draught—the great desideratum in building long chimneys, which is prevented taking place (the equilibrium) by its being rarefied by combustion in passing through the furnace.

"Suppose, after the flue was filled with smoke and rarefied air, the communication from the furnace was cut off by a damper, and another one opened for the atmosphere to pass into the flue, would there not be a very strong draught into

it, intense at first, and progressively diminishing till an equilibrium was effected?
The malt kiln has large flues or chambers
under the perforated tiles, into which the
hot air generated in the fire passes, and,
without the aid of any chimney, has a
strong draught.

" The baker's oven, when heated by a
fire in what they designate a wagon, has
a very strong draught, entirely owing to
the space the smoke and hot air has to
spread in, before passing to the chimney.
The same oven, when heated by a fire
spread on the bottom in the common
way, has a very poor draught, the oven
being converted into a fire-place without
any hot-air chambers or large horizontal
flue. The reason why the wagon plan is
not in more general use, is owing to the
wagon being so soon burnt out, arising
from the strong draught. It is an almost
universally received opinion that horizontal flues check a draught ; but this, I conceive, arises from their being generally
made of the same size as the flue of the
chimney.

Have not some of the recent builders of long chimneys, to supersede several smaller ones, planted them at some distance from their furnaces, and made a horizontal flue to carry all their draughts to the chimney? and when they have turned the first draught into it they have had a very strong one ; but as they have added the others, the draught has progressively diminished. The width of the large chimney is made too large for one draught, consequently the atmosphere would descend the chimney and create a down-draught, diminishing the advantage of its height for one draught ; but as the rest of the draughts were put in, the down-draught would be less and less, and when all were put in, the smoke and hot air would fill the chimney to the top, having the whole benefit which its elevation is supposed to give,—demonstrating, as I conceive, that the horizontal flue, which was constructed wide for several flues to run into, is the occasion of the superior draught, when only one was put in, and not the long chimney.

" As respects the smoke when it is passing through the proposed flue, from the great space it has to pass in, it moves slowly along, though the draught is quick. From this circumstance, and the rarefaction of the air in it, he conceives it will have time to condense and fall to the bottom of the flue before it arrives at the chimney. But to render this desirable object more complete, he thinks that if the condensing water from the engine was introduced by a siphon pipe into the flue next to the furnace, and passed along its whole length in a gutter, and taken out near the chimney by another siphon pipe, the steam that would arise from the water would partly be absorbed by the floating particles of soot, and sooner fall to the bottom.

"The writer some time ago, erected a flue, or chambers, similar to what he has described, to destroy coal tar. He set fire to a quantity of shavings in the flue, and then lighted the coal tar in the fireplace, calculating that it would burn slowly, and that the soot would all be deposited at the bottom of the flue. When ignited, it blazed most furiously, and passed through the small into the large flue with such rapidity, owing to the intense draught, and the flame was carried such a distance in, that the chamber would soon have been destroyed, being covered with flags, that he had it put out as expeditiously as possible. He then had small low arches built over the fire-place, leaving out a brick here and there, by which means he checked the draught, which was still sufficiently strong for the purpose, and not a particle of soot issued from the chimney, all being deposited at the bottom of the flue. The chimney, if it could be so called, was not more than eighteen inches high, and not more than three feet above the level of the flue from the fire-place.

(Signed) "A CONSTANT READER."

The writer of the foregoing letter was a well-known engineer in Manchester, and at the time of its publication, his opinions on the subject treated on were highly valued by several of the manufacturers, who placed the matter in my hands for the purpose of investigation, and the result was the following letter addressed to the editor of the same paper:

"The proposal of your correspondent for attaching long horizontal flues or chambers to steam-engine furnaces, if carried into effect, so far from serving as a substitute for long chimneys, would render them more than ever necessary. Nothing can be better established among practical men conversant with the subject than the fact, that every interruption or bend in the flue of a furnace acts as a check to the draught, and where such checks or interruptions occur, there is generally found a deposit of soot or dust, which otherwise would have found its way through the flue and out at the chimney top.

"With respect to the strong draughts generally obtained at a malt-kiln or a baker's oven, very little consideration is required to see that the draught in such cases depends upon quite a different principle to that of a steam-engine fur-

nace. In those, the draught is, in great
part, owing to the great mass of brickwork and other materials (generally substances that retain heat a long time)
used in their construction, becoming
heated to a considerable degree at the
commencement, and from which, by the
nature of the operations carried on, the
heat is but slowly abstracted. Hence
the velocity of the current of air passing
through the furnace is accelerated in
proportion to the length of the flues, or
area of heated surface, and a very small
chimney is therefore sufficient. Whereas, in the case of a steam-engine boiler,
things are very different, for here we
have the fire generally surrounded by an
extensive surface of iron plate, kept comparatively cool by the contained water
rapidly abstracting the heat in the generation of steam. And, in order that this
abstraction of the heat by the water
should be as complete as possible, before
the smoke is allowed to pass off into the
chimney, numberless contrivances have
been resorted to; as is exemplified in the

multiflue **boiler of** Messrs. Booth and Stephenson, to the **application** of which to locomotive purposes, we are undoubtedly indebted for the only efficient system **of economical traveling by** railway.

"**You must** easily perceive, **that with any** regard to economy especially, how important it is in the generation of steam, that the smoke should leave the boiler at a comparatively low temperature; and if so, its tendency **to ascend must be very small;** particularly when you recollect **that** carbonic acid, **which is** one of the **principal** products **of** the combustion of **coal, is** considerably heavier than **atmospheric** air of the same temperature. **Hence** exists the absolute necessity of assisting the draught by the superior levity of a column of heated air, as compared **to** that of a similar column of the **external** atmosphere, **the** pressure of **which, by a well-known** hydrostatical **law, is in a** certain direct ratio to its perpendicular height, and is quite independent of its other dimensions.

"It requires no theoretical elucidation,

and very little scientific knowledge, to
understand **the great** difference there is
in principle between the firing of a steam-
engine boiler and the heating of a baker's
oven. Almost **any one, I should think,
who** pays common attention to such subjects must be aware of it; and the same
may be said of a gas retort furnace, or of
a brick-kiln. In these it is the mass of
non-conducting matter heated, and the
slow abstraction **of this** heat, leaving a
large surplus **to pass** up the chimney,
which is the principal cause of draught.
On the contrary, in the furnace **of a**
steam-engine boiler, the largest possible
quantity of heating surface (but as re-
gards its effects on the draught it may
more properly be called cooling surface),
composed of the best conducting sub-
stance, is, **or** ought to be, exposed to the
current of hot air; consequently the
main flues and chimneys of such furnaces
are nearly as cool as the external atmosphere. Therefore, unless an artificial
blast is used, as in the locomotives and
some other high-pressure engines, the

adoption of long chimneys is altogether unavoidable.

"If manufacturers who employ steam-engines were at all likely to be induced to increase so important an item of their expenditure as that of fuel, for the mere purpose of heating their chimneys—which is evidently the principle of your correspondent's scheme—it might be worth while showing him that the great desideratum of smoke burning would thereby be rendered more difficult of attainment than ever. Of this, indeed any one who admits the facts, which all must do—that for burning or preventing smoke we require an increased heat of the fire, and for increasing the heat of the fire we require an increased draught through the fire, rather than through the flue—it is only necessary to observe what takes place when a chimney is on fire, to be convinced of what I now state. In such case the draught is all in the flue instead of the fire-place, where it ought to be; and, of course, the heat is then all at the wrong end of the chimney.

" That checking the draught of a furnace by brickwork or other obstructions in the flues, may be termed a preventive of smoke, is admitted—partly by causing a deposit of soot in the flues, but principally from the smoke not being so rapidly generated. In the latter particular it bears some resemblance to many other plans strongly recommended in your and other papers for years past, as I have no doubt many other similar plans will, for good and substantial reasons, independent of their merits or demerits, continue to be recommended for years to come. The principle of all the plans we are alluding to is the same, and equivalent to the notable expedient of keeping the furnace door open until the fire ceases to smoke. In other words, they amount, in the generality of cases, to a complete conversion of the furnace, for a time, to the condition of a common open house-fire. Of course, under such circumstances, the prevention of much smoke becomes a very easy matter, for very little is generated; and owing to the same circumstances, I must also add, very little steam !

(Signed)

"An Advocate for Long Chimneys."

EXAMPLES OF ENGINE CHIMNEYS.

The Mayfield Experimental Chimneys.—The original design for the proportions and dimensions of this chimney were made by the author for the well-known firm of Thomas Hoyle & Sons, the eminent calico printers of Manchester, and the chimney was erected for them by the equally well-known builders, Messrs. David Bellhouse & Sons, of that city, several years ago. Its total cost, including the foundation, which was 10 ft. deep, by 15 ft. square at the bottom, very little exceeded £100.

The shaft of this chimney is octagonal in plan, about 2 ft. 10½ in. wide externally at the top, and 5 ft. at bottom. It stands on a pedestal of 8 ft. square, which together with the shaft make up a total height of 90 ft. from the ground—that being the lowest elevation allowed by the police regulations of the then borough of Manchester. The whole height from the base of the foundation being 100 ft., and about 88 ft. from the level of the fire-grate, which is the proper datum line from which all calculations respecting the draught is to be taken. The whole, excepting the stone cap and cornice, being of brickwork.

The shaft has a batter, externally of one inch to the yard, which is the usual rate, in this part of Lancashire. In the northern and hilly parts of the country—say about Preston and Oldham—a batter of one and a quarter inch to the yard is more generally used.

The work at the bottom of the shaft is 19 in. thick, and that of the top is 9 in. The shaft is entirely octagonal inside throughout down to the bottom, and externally to the top of the pedestal.

The internal capacity of the chimney, together with the short flue connecting it with the boiler, to which it is attached, is about 50 cubic yards.

The internal horizontal area of the narrowest part of the aperture at the top of the chimney is about 1,000 sq. in., which, as it was intended to make the chimney large enóugh for about 50 horse power, gives about 20 sq. in. area for each horse power; while, as above stated, there was about one cubic yard capacity in the chimney for the same.

Although the proportion of 20 sq. in. area of chimney aperture, for each horse power of a steam-engine, had been generally accounted in Lancashire to be "according to Boulton and Watt," neither that nor the proportion of a cubic yard of capacity per horse power was adopted from any theoretical rule or previously determined opinion, excepting that they were nearly the average of some of the best chimneys we were then well acquainted with. For, although Tredgold's rule had been published a few years previously, and was generally considered to be founded on principles pretty nearly correct, it was very evident that author himself had not sufficient knowledge of the working of steam-engines to enable him to obtain proper **constants** for the **practical application of** his **own** calculations, simple **and** admirable as **the latter generally were.** There only, in fact, **wanted a more careful** selection of data to render **his formulæ highly** valuable to the practical engine-maker.

The **proprietors** of the Mayfield Print-**works—the** intimate friends, disciples and **patrons of the** celebrated John Dalton, **the great reformer of chemistry, who** was **at the time of these experiments,** as he **had been for some** years previously, our constant **visitor and adviser** in scientific matters—**were not the kind** of men to be easily led **astray by** Tredgold's, or any **other mere** theoretical rules about steam-engines, **however flourishing** the algebra by which they might **be** surrounded. They had in fact wisely **resolved** to erect **this** experimental chimney for the very purpose of acquiring for themselves ac-**curate experimental** knowledge and **correct** practical data in all that relates to chimneys and boilers; including also, though not at the time, an essential objec, a little smoke burning by the way; in all of which, not only Tredgold, but most other theoretical writers on the steam-engine, appeared to them clearly deficient.

On referring to Tredgold's rule, in his well-known work "The Steam Engine," we found him recommending what rendered his authority entirely nugatory in the matter of chimneys—namely, that "a chimney of double the size given by the rule should be built;" and, as if conscious of the great inconsistency—to say the least—of giving us this kind of instruction, he adds the following very lame reason: "because the expense," he states, "bears a small ratio to the increase of size, and it may afterwards be convenient if considerably larger than is necessary for the engine it is erected for?" Now, although Tredgold, justly or unjustly, up to that time had stood foremost in the application of high mathematical acquirements to the improvement of the steam-engine, advice of this kind necessarily demolished all confidence in his book as a scientific guide on the subject of chimneys.

The extract above quoted from Tredgold is followed up by an example in which the side of a square chimney for a 40-horse engine is calculated to be equal to 23 in. "But" he adds, "I would advise to build a chimney 33 in. square!"

The rule and the example, as given in Woolhouse's edition of Tredgold's work (Art. 275), published in 1833, after the author's death, are as follows:

"RULE—The area of a chimney in inches, for a low-pressure steam engine, when above 10 horse power, should be 112 times the horse power of the engine, divided by the square root of the height of the chimney in feet.

"EXAMPLE—Required the area of a chimney for an engine of 40-horse power, the height of it being 70 ft.

"In this case

$$\frac{40 \times 112}{\sqrt{70}} = \frac{4480}{8.4} = 533.2 \text{ sq. in.}$$

"The square root of this is 23 in., which

will be the side of a square chimney. Or, multiply 533 by 1.27, and extract the square root for the diameter of a circular one."

Now, as my present purpose is the practical one of showing how a chimney for the furnace of a steam-engine boiler ought to be built, and what are its proportions, in order best to answer the object in view, namely, the obtainment of a good draught with stability and economy—I shall, at least in the first instance, purposely waive all theoretical refinements of calculation until a rough outline of the method of proceeding be fairly established. To effect this in the most simple and direct manner, I depend far more on practice than theory, on example rather than precept—a mode of proceedure analogous to that of teaching any common mechanical trade, which I have occasionally resorted to on other subjects, with a certain measure of success.

In Weale's large edition of "Tredgold on the Steam Engine," in 4 quarto volumes, 1852, edited up to page 116, by the late Professor James Hann, of King's College, and thence up to page 308 by the present writer, I gave, in the notes, some examples of these calculations for chimneys adapted to practical data first discovered—at least, collected and arranged—by the late Joshua Milne, Esq., of Shaw, near Oldham, some years prior to the first publication of Tredgold's work, in which the area of the chimney is expressed in square feet instead of inches. Adapting Tredgold's rule to Mr. Milne's data, it only requires the constant multiplier 112 to be substituted by 280, and the calculation in the above case will then stand as follows:

$$\frac{40 \times 280}{\sqrt{70}} = \frac{11,200}{8.4} = 1,333 \text{ sq. in.}$$

instead of 533; a result nearly three times as much as that obtained by Tredgold, and the square root of which is $36\frac{1}{2}$ in. for the side of the square chimney, instead of 23 in., as before. That is to say, about 3 ft. and 2 ft. square, respectively.

It is obviously much better to simplify

such practical rules as these, by using
the same denomination for both dimensions, the height and the area, or the
diameter of the chimney. And since the
large expensive edition of Tredgold as
above referred to, as published by Weale,
which has been until recently in a great
measure a sealed book to many practical
men, is now in the hands of a more
liberal and enterprising publisher, who
has made it more accessible by reducing
it to less than one-half its former price,
we have some pleasure in promoting its
utility in the same direction, by adding
here, as was partially attempted in that
work, a formula which includes Milne's
constant, for ready computation by in-
strumental inspection, as well as by common arithmetic, so that every intelligent
operative who honors these pages by his
perusal and carries a slide rule, has always
at hand a ready mode of verifying the
truth of our statements, and comparing
them with those of Tredgold, or any
other authority.

SLIDE-RULE FORMULA FOR HORSE POWER OF
CHIMNEYS.

A	Area in inches.	Con-stants.	Tredgold 112
ꓛ	sq.root of height in ft.	Nom. H. Power.	Milne... 280

Tredgold's **example** for a 40-horse engine **before** referred to:

A	Area $=533$ in.	Tredgold's Cons. $=112$
ꓛ	$\sqrt{70}=8.4$ ft.	Nom. H. P. $= 40$

Milne's Const. $=280$
Nom. H. P. $= \overline{16}$

In his arithmetical rule, instead of a multiplier, Milne used a divisor for a constant number, and was in words as follows:

RULE.—Multiply the square root of the height of the chimney in feet, by the square of its internal diameter at its top or narrowest part also in feet, and half the product will be the nominal horsepower that the chimney is equal to.

Taking the same example as before, it is by arithmetic—

$$\frac{\sqrt{70} \times (1 \text{ ft. } 11 \text{ in., or}) 1 \cdot 92^2}{\text{divided by } 2} = \frac{8.4 \times 3.68}{2} = 15 \cdot 45$$

horse **power;** and by the slide rule it is *approximately—*

A | Diam. | $^2 = 3.68$ Cons. divisor 2

C | $\sqrt{}$height $= 8\ 4$ | Horse power $= 15.4$

After we first published these chimney
rules, at the desire of **Mr.** Milne, several
years ago, apprising him at the time of
the wide difference between his and
Tredgold's results, we soon found, and he
admitted, that a somewhat smaller proportion of chimney area would be more
nearly in accordance with the general
practice throughout the country, more
especially where a better quality of coal
was burned than that ordinarily used at
the factories in Oldham, where, from the
peculiar quality of the cotton manufacture
carried on there—spinning coarse cotton,
waste, and shoddy—a larger measure of
work was usually allowed for a nominal
horse power than elsewhere. In fact,
two indicated horse-power for one nominal was then the regular Oldham measure
for steam-engines.

If we take Tredgold's advice, and give
double the area of chimney-top obtained
by his rule, then the adoption of $1\frac{1}{2}$ instead of **2** for a constant divisor will give

that result which we may conveniently call the actual instead of the nominal, or Oldham horse power, which will still, as it ought, be considerably in excess of the indicated power of steam-engines in general.

In illustration of this, take—

Example 2.—Required the number of horse power most suitable in connection with the experimental chimney at Mayfield already described; the height above the level of the fire-bars being 88 ft., and the inside diameter at the top 2 ft. $10\frac{1}{2}$ in.

SOLUTION BY SLIDE-RULE.

(Slide inverted as before).

A | Diam. 2 ft. $10\frac{1}{2}$ in. | $^2 = 2.87^2 = 8.26$
O | $\sqrt{\text{ht.}}$ (88) $= 9.38$

New Const. $= 1\ 15$
Answer 51 H. P.

Example 3.—Another new chimney erected the same year, in the same works (Thomas Hoyle & Sons), was $3\frac{1}{2}$ ft. diameter by 40 yards high. Required the horse power it is equal to.

SOLUTION.

A | Diam. 3½ ft. | $^2 = 12\frac{1}{4}$ | Const. number 1½
O | √ht. (120) = 11 | Horse power 90

The chimney in this example (3) was erected in November of the same year, and by the same builder as that in Example 2. It was built with similar materials in the same manner like the preceding chimney. The shaft was octagonal, but higher in proportion to its area than the former, for the purpose of carrying away the smoke from contact with some adjacent buildings, and the cost was about double that of the experimental chimney. By which it will be seen that we had arrived at a fair average cost of chimney.building in proportion to the power capable of being produced in that way, so far as chimneys of this character, and from 30 to 40 yards high, are concerned—namely, about £2 per horse power.

The very many practical tests of various kinds that were applied to these two chimneys, during several successive years, such as finding that the second chimney

was equally applicable to two as the first
or experimental chimney was to one boiler of similar size, not much over or under
45 or 50 horse power each, convinced us
that we had approximated near to the
data we were in quest of.

The Duckinfield Bleach **Works,** *Chimney and* **Furnaces.**—The subject of our
next example in chimney building serves
still further to corroborate our Mayfield
experiments in all respects except as to
cost, which of course greatly diminished
as the scale of our operations became
larger.

This chimney was erected early in the
spring of the year following the comple-
tion of those last named, at Messrs.
Hoyle & Sons' New Bleach Works, then
erecting at Sandy Lane, between Duckinfield and Staleybridge.

In the planning of the chimney and
flues, and furnishing the designs, with all
their details, and four large boilers, for
which the writer was more especially en-
gaged, and which were expected to furnish
from **200** to 300 horse power of steam,

we had the valuable assistance of Mr. John Graham,* afterwards a member of the firm, and whose eminent talents as a scientific and practical chemist are generally known—as we also previously had the cordial assistance, general concurrence and approval of the late Mr. Alfred Binyon, the then managing partner.

Example 4.—The Duckenfield Bleach Works chimney was made **45** yards high by 6 ft. inside diameter at the top. Required the horse power it is equal to.

SOLUTION.

A	Diam. 6 ft.	$^2 = 36$ New constant $= 1\frac{1}{2}$
0	√ht. (135 ft.) $= 11.6$	Horse power $= 278$

Milne's Const.　2

" " 208

* See a valuable paper by this gentleman in vol. xv. of the "Transactions of the Literary and Philosophical Society of Manchester," for the years 1857-8. A portion of it was also republished in the *Engineer* newspaper for March 12, 1858, which gave an account of a series of evaporating experiments, made for the purpose of testing the economy of fuel and management effected at these boilers and furnaces through a series of successive years, which will well repay perusal, and will be further adverted to in a subsequent part or appendix to this work.

The above slide-rule solution for the power of this chimney gives two answers to the question—namely, 278 and 208 horse power, respectively, according as the new constant 1½, or Milne's old constant 2, are used as gauge points. In this case the latter was preferred, as giving the most correct result, by reason of the kind of fuel intended to be consumed being of the same or similar inferior quality to that already referred to as being in general use within the parish of Oldham, to which these works were nearly adjoining. Facility in obtaining this cheap fuel—known as "burgey" and "slack"—being one of the chief reasons for erecting the works in this particular locality.

THE EXPERIMENTAL BOILERS.

In the collection of data for steam-engine chimneys, it would be a great omission to leave out the particular dimensions of the boiler, to cause the efficient working of which is, in fact, the only profitable work the chimney has to do.

The boiler, for which the Mayfield experimental chimney was erected, was designed by the writer, as was also the chimney, as already stated, specially for experimental purposes, in acquiring all practical information on the subject previous to commencing the construction of Messrs. Hoyle & Sons' new Bleaching and Calico-printing Works at Duckinfield, near Staleybridge. For this purpose I did not hesitate to recommend the plainest and simplest form of boiler that can be conceived—namely, a plain cylinder, laid horizontally, or nearly so, with the fire to go underneath it at one end, and out to the chimney at the other, which may now be described.

This experimental boiler was of the " direct draught" kind, that is, without return flues, and this one had no flues of any kind, either inside or out. The boiler and chimney were, therefore, both of the simplest possible kind, and for that reason made mutual tests of their respective capabilities through a long series of very accurate experiments relative to economy of fuel, as well as to the efficiency of various methods of smoke prevention, or smoke burning, as it was then popularly termed, and other matters of interest to the proprietors. Improvements in smoke prevention especially were freely invited from all quarters, and this was the boiler at which very many different plans for the purpose were tried.

This kind of boiler was fully described in the author's "Essay on the Boilers of Steam Engines" (1839), and the principal dimensions of this one, as there given, need only be shortly referred to here. It was in shape cylindrical, and fully equal to 30 horse power, being $33\frac{1}{2}$ ft. long by $5\frac{1}{2}$ diameter, and " set up," or rather hung, by means of cast-iron brackets riveted to the sides, and resting on the side walls of the furnace, so that the whole of the lower half of its convex surface, about 32 square yards, was exposed to the direct action of the fire and flame.

The fire-grate, placed about 22 in. below the bottom of the boiler, was $5\frac{1}{2}$ ft. square, or equal to about 30 sq. ft. in area, and was composed of one length of fire-bars, each $1\frac{3}{4}$ in. thick on the face, with air-spaces of $\frac{5}{16}$ to $\frac{3}{8}$ of an inch wide between them.

This boiler supplied steam to an old Boulton and Watt condensing engine of 16-horse power, by Messrs. Sherratt, of Salford, loaded so as to require seldom less than 24 cubic feet of water to be evaporated per hour at a pressure of exactly 4 lbs. per sq. in. It also supplied steam for heating drying cylinders, for boiling water, and for a great variety of other purposes, amounting at times to nearly as much as the engine required itself. The least average evaporation for a whole day together .was 33, and the greatest 45 cubic feet per hour. The lower amount was, of course, obtained at the most economical rate, namely, at about 6 lbs. of water evaporated for each pound of common coal burned. It was, therefore, considered to be full 30-horse power. A cubic foot of water evaporated per hour, being generally considered amply sufficient to supply steam for each horse power (nominal) of a Boulton and Watt or low-pressure engine in good order, however it might be at times over-loaded.

Although this evaporation of a cubic foot, or a little over six imperial gallons of water, of 10 lbs. each, is what boiler-makers have universally, and practical engineers commonly, agreed to consider nominally a boiler horse power, there is no doubt, however, that the same weight of water, as steam, at a higher pressure can easily be, and is frequently, made to work two or three indicated horse power in a modern steam-engine, accordingly as the latter is arranged to work to a greater or less extent expansively.

This boiler was made of Low Moor iron $\frac{5}{16}$ in. thick, except the bottom row of plates, which were $\frac{3}{8}$ in. and the flat ends $\frac{7}{16}$, by Mr. Fairbairn, of Manchester, who had just previously commenced the boiler-making business, and was then a staunch advocate for introducing the long

Cornish high-pressure boiler, with its one
large internal furnace-flue, and single fur-
nace-grate. **Instead of that kind of**
boiler, **now much less used, except in**
Wales and Cornwall, **I persisted in advis-**
ing the simple and elementary form of
boiler now described. It was also sus-
pended by bracket flanges in **the cheap**
and simple manner above mentioned, **in**
accordance with the universal dogma **of**
its strictly utilitarian owners, **which in**
this, as in all other business **matters con-**
nected with the works, was never **lost**
sight of for **a** moment,—in **order** that
any alterations or improvements that
might be found expedient, either in the
construction of the boiler, or **erection of**
the brick-work, might be in the shape **of**
additions merely, and therefore **capable**
of being separately **proved, both as to**
first cost and utility, and also **that our**
experiments might be carried **on for a**
sufficient **length of** time, **without** the
usual liability to interruption **from the**
necessity of cleaning out **of** flues **or**
otherwise.

The last-mentioned particular in the erection of this boiler was of considerable importance in thus attaining the main object we had in view, as well as in accomplishing another object greatly desired by the benevolent proprietors of the works, that of doing away with the degrading practice of sweeping out the flues by means of men, or rather boys, crawling through them.

Trifling as a small matter of this kind may appear to some, it is important to show that, in this instance at least, it was attended by considerable economy Cast-iron lugs or brackets, with broad flanges, were riveted along each side of the boiler, a little above the intended surface level of the water, and these brackets rested on the tops of the two vertical side walls of the furnace and flame-bed. The boiler thus suspended between the two side walls was then adjusted, not quite horizontally, but slightly inclined, with a fall of about 8 in. towards the front end, so that a greater proportion of the water was brought immediately over the fire-grate.

This arrangement of the flame-bed and seating, or side walls, of the boiler, formed a chamber or receptacle, large enough to hold all the flue-dust and dirt that could be found from the use of any kind of coal whatever, for a considerable time. In fact, although the boiler was every day at work, the flame-bed did not require any cleaning out, even at the end of nearly two years,—when, as an opportunity occurred, several cart-loads of flue-dust were removed from under the boiler at one time. The occasion of having this operation performed, discovered to us a circumstance, which is sometimes the cause of great disappointment to the expectations of parties who, for the first time, have boilers erected on this direct draught plan, which requires an explanation in this place.

At all direct draught boilers, it is usual to have, and highly necessary that there should be, two or more transverse "check" or flame-bridges, in addition to the ordinary fire bridge, carried up to within 6 or 7 in. of the boiler bottom; but in this case, there was, in the first instance, only one of these additional bridges, and the man employed to get out the flue-dust had, in order to make an easier passage . for himself, removed two or three courses of brick-work from the top of the flame-bridge, and neglected to replace them again. The consequence was, that on the boiler commencing work again, a clear loss of 15 per cent. in fuel was detected immediately, besides the overheating of the damper-plate and brickwork of the chimney entrance, which evils were, of course, quickly rectified by replacing the brickwork. Although no very great nicety is required in adjusting the height of these flame-bridges, and an inch or two higher or lower may not make much difference in the economy of fuel; but the extent of 8 or 9 in. in depth of the air passage over them, when there is already a depth of the same extent in the throat area over the furnace-bridge, will at any time cause an exorbitant waste of fuel.

The fact of an error of this kind, which is very liable to be passed over unnoticed by ordinary bricklayers and boiler-setters, unless very carefully supervised, has been frequently the occasion of much error in experiments on the economy of fuel. It is all the more necessary to mention the above circumstances here, because, since my description of the direct draught method of setting boilers was first published in 1837-8, I have occasionally had complaints from parties who had been induced to adopt the direct plan, but had not succeeded in realizing any moderate measure of economy therefrom, and had, in consequence, too readily, or without sufficient examination, given it up, and returned again to the wheel-draught, narrow flue system, with its little army of chimney-sweeps, boiler-menders, and laborers, and all its other disagreeable and expensive accompaniments of Sunday work, over-work, and night-work. It is, however, but fair to state that extreme

cases of this kind have been mostly con-
fined to the South of England and the
metropolis, where the extravagant use of
flaming Newcastle or Hartley coal, with
very much unnecessary stoking of the
fires, is still continued. These results
have been helped not a little, perhaps, by
the prognostications of many of the old
school of bricklayers, that the direct
draught plan would " send all the heat
up the chimney," and who too often tes-
tify their sincerity in such a belief by taking special care to build their chimneys
and flues very narrow and very crooked.
The prejudices of some of the attend-
ants of engines in London in favor of
much stoking and hard firing, which is
literally working hard at wasting coal,
are difficult to account for, especially
when found among persons not notori-
ous for working hard at anything else ;
but a residence among them of any one
whose business is to save fuel, will very soon
convince him of the fact. Hence a more
careful attention to the condition of all

the bridges under a boiler is a necessity which ought never **to be neglected.**

1. Engineers and firemen who would keep steam with economy, should do with as little stoking **or** stirring of the fire as possible, if any. In order to do so, they should see before starting that the furnace is properly constructed for the purpose, and large enough for the quantity of steam required. The fire-grate should have about **1 sq. ft. of** effective fire-bar surface **for each nominal** horse-power **of** the engine, or for each cubic foot **of** water required to **be** boiled away per hour. The **fire-bars** may be from $\frac{1}{2}$ to $\frac{3}{4}$ **in.** thick on the face with $\frac{1}{4}$ to $\frac{3}{8}$ in. draught spaces bet**ween** them, and with joggles to **keep them asunder** nearly the whole **depth of the bar.** The boiler should **have, at least, 8 or 10 sq.** ft. of heating **surface per horse, and the** chimney should be of sufficient capacity to create a draught into the furnace equal to the pressure of **a column of** water $\frac{3}{8}$

to ⅜ in. deep, when the damper is set wide open.

2. In firing, spread the large and small coals (equally mixed) on all parts of the grate, thicker at the back of the grate near the bridge than at the front, because the draught is there the strongest, and the coals burn away the quickest.

3. The fire should never be less than about 3 or four inches thick in the middle of its length, 2 or 3 in. in front, and 6 or 8 in. at the back of the grate. In no case should the fire exceed double the depth here stated; and never more than two-thirds of the fire-grate should be entirely covered with fresh coals at one time.

4. If a regularly uniform supply of steam is required and the damper quite up, the quantity of fuel on the grate may be gradually increased; but when an increasing quantity of steam is wanted, the average thickness or quantity of fuel on the grate must not then be increased, but ought rather to be diminished, and supplied by smaller quantities at a time,

and more frequently. So soon, however, as the supply of steam exceeds the demand, **the coal** must again be supplied by larger quantities at a time, regularly increasing **the** quantity of fuel in the grate as before. On the other hand, when a diminished supply of steam is required, **close** the damper a little, and take the opportunity of levelling the fire or cleaning the fire-bars, doing one-half of the grate at a time.

5. A steam-engine furnace worked **in** this way will make very little smoke; or, if any, it may be prevented when desirable by opening the fire-door 2 or 3 in. for 1 or 2 min. after each firing. Bearing in mind that the production of steam is commonly lessened by doing so, but so is **the consumption** of the fuel.

6. **Stokers** should understand that they are not to make a business of "stoking," but to leave it off entirely, excepting only when preparing to clear out the grate from clinkers and rubbish, which requires to be done generally three or four times a day with average qualities of

coal; convenient times being chosen for **the** purpose when there is the least demand for steam.

7. A fireman's business is, first, to see, before the fire-door is opened, that no **coal is left in** the heap ready for going on bigger than a man**'s** fist; and that very small coal or slack **is wetted, or at** least damp, as well as a little water **always** in the ashpit. Then **begin by** charging **into the** farther end **of the furnace,** reaching **to** about one-third **the length of the** grate from the bridge, **as** rapidly as possible, from **a** dozen to twenty or thirty **spadefuls** of coals, **until they** form **a bank** reaching nearly or quite up to the top of the bridge, and then shut the fire-door, until the other **fires, if there are any, are** served in the **same way.**

8. In firing up, **throw the coals** over the rest of the grate by scattering them evenly from **side to side, but** thinner **at** the front, near the dead **plate, than at the middle or back. In this manner keep the** fuel moderately thick **and** level across the bars, but always thicker **at the** back than

the front, not by pushing the fire in, but by throwing the coals on exactly where they are wanted.

9. Never for a moment leave any portion of the bars uncovered, which must be prevented by throwing or pitching a spadeful of coals right into any hollow or thin place that appears; and always remember that three or four spadefuls thrown quickly one on the top of the other, will make no more smoke than one, and generally less. But all depends on doing it quickly; that being the main, if not the only point in which freedom from smoke and economy of fuel agree. Some firemen only put on three spadefuls, while another can put on four, and make 20 per cent. more steam in the same time by doing it.

10. In replenishing the fire, take every opportunity of keeping up the bank of fuel at the bridge, by re-charging it, one side at a time. Whenever this bank is burnt entirely through, or low, and also when the fire is in a low state generally, take the rake and draw back the half-

burnt fuel, 12 or 18 in. from the bridge, and re-charge fresh coal into its place, upon the bare fire-bars as at first.

11. An engine fire tended in this way will consume its own smoke without difficulty, simply by admitting a very moderate supply of air (which for safety to the boiler should be heated) at the bridge, this being a more certain and economical mode of prevention than that of diluting the smoke by the admission of much cold air at the fire-doors.

12. It may be set down as an axiom that a steam-engine chimney cannot be too large, if only provided with a damper, although ninety-nine in one hundred, at the present time, are decidedly too small. They are unable to create a sufficient draught of air through the furnace, consequently a smoky flame is produced, instead of a flame with little or no smoke.

13. Want of chimney draught is a defect which no smoke-consuming furnace in the world can remedy, whether using hot air or cold, unless by the application

of an artificial blast, which commonly costs as much to work as the heat it creates is worth.

14. It being impossible to consume smoke without great heat, which requires a good draught, and difficult to get a good draught without a large chimney, I here set down a table of chimney proportions, which have been practically proved to answer well with the inferior steam coal of the manufacturing and midland districts for many years past. It is true that some-what smaller dimensions might serve where the extravagant use of Newcastle coal is still continued, as in London; but even here those dimensions and proportions ought to be adhered to, because of the constant tendency to increase the engine and boiler power, while the same brick chimney remains. For similar reasons I commence with a chimney suitable for a 10-horse boiler, although a five, or even a 2-horse engine only, may be required.

Height of Chimney.	Inside Diameter at Top.	Nominal Horse-power of boiler.
20 yards	1 ft. 6 in.	10
25 "	1 " 8 "	12
30 "	1 " 10 "	16
33 "	2 " 0 "	20
35 "	2 " 6 "	30
40 "	3 " 0 "	50
40 "	3 " 6 "	70
40 "	4 " 0 "	90
45 "	4 " 6 "	120
50 "	5 " 0 "	160
55 "	5 " 6 "	200
60 "	6 " 0 "	250

15. A common low-pressure condensing engine is usually overloaded when it has less than 25 circular in. in the cylinder for each nominal horse-power; and a high-pressure non-condensing engine ought to have from 10 to $12\frac{1}{2}$, and to be worked at double the effective pressure, at the least, of the former,—say 30 to 40 lbs. per square inch in the boiler.

DIMENSIONS

—OF—

TALL CHIMNEYS.

By L. PINZGER.

DIMENSIONS OF TALL CHIMNEYS.

———• ••———

THE formula frequently employed for the determination of the height of a chimney is:

$$u_a = \varphi \sqrt{2gh \frac{T_m - T_o}{T_o}},$$

in which U_a is the velocity of the escaping gases; $T_o = 273 + t_o$, the absolute temperature of the exterior air; $T_m = 273 + t_m$, the absolute mean temperature of the gases in the chimney (t_o and t_m being expressed in centigrade degrees); $g = 9.81$, the acceleration of gravity, and φ a coefficient of correction relating to the resistances opposed to the motion of heated gases.

M. Grashoff, in 1866, propounded a theory which renders it easy to take account of the causes which modify the movements of the products of combustion; more recently he has introduced a *résumé* of this theory in his work, *Construction des Machines.*

While the results thus obtained are mathematically accurate, they have not yet taken a convenient form for practical use; partly because the principles of the mechanical theory of heat have not been generally adapted to the calculation of the movement of gases, and partly in consequence of the complex character of the formulas.

Thus the height h of the chimney cannot be deduced directly in terms of the other quantities; it is necessary to resort to approximate methods. In order to simplify the calculations, M. Grashof has constructed tables adapted for use in the case of chimnies and temperatures such as are commonly employed in practice. He has also established easy empirical formulas deduced from exact theory.

The writer proposes to briefly review the principles involved, and then to develop a method of calculation which shall possess the precision of Prof

Grashof's, but which will afford an easy practical formula.

The special function of a chimney is to cause a sufficient quantity of air to traverse the mass of fuel spread over the grate to insure its combustion—to make the hot gases circulate through conduits where they part with a portion of their heat—and finally to discharge these gases into the atmosphere with a velocity which shall diminish as much as possible the action of the wind upon the draft.

When the products of combustion are deleterious to health or vegetation, it becomes necessary to employ high chimneys, so that these products shall reach the earth only after being mixed with a large volume of air.

The cause of the draft lies in the difference of pressure in the gases in the fire, the flues, the shaft and that of the outside air at the level of the grate.

Let p_0 be the atmospheric pressure in kilograms per square meter at the level of the grate; p_1, p_2, p_3 and p_4 the pressures in the fire, at the entrance to the flue; at the outlet from the flue; in the horizontal shaft and at the base of the chimney; then we ought to have $p_0 > p_1 > p_2 > p_3 > p_4$ so as to insure draft.

It is necessary then, 1st, to obtain such a pressure p_4 at the base of the chimney as would be produced by a current of air required for the combustion; and 2d, to force the gas to the height of the chimney and discharge it with sufficient velocity.

The difference of pressure $p_0 - p_1$ cannot be determined by theory alone, but the direct measure of it is obtained by the manometer. In stationary furnaces this difference corresponds to a water column of 3 to 20 millimeters, according to the thickness of the layer of fuel. In locomotives it may be as high as 100 millimeters. As the weight of a column of water having a base of one square meter and a height of one millimeter is one kilogram, it follows that $p_0 - p_1$ may be equal from 3 to 20 kilograms per square meter.

If we let h_0 represent the height of a column of air of the temperature T_0 of which the weight upon one square meter of base is $p_0 - p_1$, we shall have

$$(1) \qquad h_0 = RT_0 \log. \left(\frac{p_0}{p_1} \right)$$

R expressing the constant of the equation of gaseous condition, $pv = RT$. R being equal to 29.3 for atmospheric air, more or less humid.

In taking $p_0 = 1000^k$ per square meter under average conditions of barometric pressure, and $T = 273 + 17 = 290$, a column of air of $h_0 = 4^m.25$ to 17^m will be equal to the pressure above mentioned.

The height h_0 will depend upon the quantity of the fuel burned in a unit of time—the thickness of the layer of fuel and upon the weight of the products of combustion.

Grashof assumes for the heat of soft coal the value $h_0 = 25 \, G_1 \Delta^2$ in which G represents the quantity of gas produced by the combustion of 1 kilogram of fuel, and Δ the thickness of the layer of fuel.

If $\mathbf{G}_l = 22$ kilograms and $\triangle = 0^m.1$, we have:

$$h_0 = 25 \times 22 \times 0.01 = 5^m.50.$$

We may by this calculation find with sufficient exactness the **values** of the differences of pressure $p_1 - p_2$, $p_2 - p_3$ and $p_3 - p_4$. Taking **into** consideration **the** relations existing **between** different systems of heating and of flues, **we find**:

$$\log\left(\frac{p_1}{p_2}\right) = \frac{1}{RT_0}(1 + \zeta_2)\frac{u_0^2}{2g} \cdot \frac{T_2}{T_0}.$$

$$\log\left(\frac{p_2}{p_5}\right) = \frac{1}{RT_0}\frac{u_0^2}{2g}$$

$$\left\{ \lambda\frac{l}{d}\left(\frac{Q}{kFT_0}\right) + \frac{T_k}{T_0}\right) - 2\frac{T_2 - T_5}{T_0}\right\}$$

and $\log\left(\frac{p_5}{p_4}\right) = \frac{1}{RT_0}\zeta_3\frac{u_0^2}{2g}\frac{T_5}{T_5}$, whence

$$RT_0\log\left(\frac{p_1}{p_4}\right) = \frac{u_0^2}{2g}\left\{ \frac{(1 + \zeta_2)T_2 + \zeta_5 T_5}{T_0}\right.$$

$$+ \lambda\frac{l}{d}\left(\frac{Q}{kFT_0} + \frac{T_k}{T_0}\right) - 2\frac{T_2 - T_5}{T_0}\right\}.$$

$RT_0 \log\frac{p_1}{p_4}$ expressing equally the height

h_1 of a column of air at the exterior temperature T_0, subjected to the pressures p_1 and p_4 upon the lower and upper bases, and of which the weight measures the pressure $p_1 - p_4$ on a square meter. Consequently

$$(2) \quad h_1 = \frac{u_0^2}{2g} \left\{ \frac{(1 + \zeta_2)T_2 + \zeta_3 T_6}{T_0} + \right.$$

$$\left. \lambda \frac{l}{d} \left(\frac{Q}{k F T_0} + \frac{T_k}{T_0} \right) - 2 \frac{T_2 - T_6}{T_0} \right\}.$$

In this equation u_0 represents the velocity with which the heated gas passes the section f of the flues if they have the temperature T_6; T_2 and T_3 are the temperatures at the escape from the flue; T_k the absolute temperature (of water in a steam boiler); l the length of the flues; d their mean diameter $= \frac{4f}{P}$; (P being the perimeter and f the section); F the heated surface of the boiler; Q the quantity of heat transmitted by this surface every hour; k the coefficient of conductivity of the surface for heat, which for boilers is about 20; ζ_2 and ζ_3 the coefficients of correction relating to the sudden changes in diameter and direction; (in steam boilers $\zeta_2 = 1.5$ to 25, and $\zeta_3 = 0.8$ to 1); λ the coefficient of friction in the flues ($= 0.08$).

Between the quantities F, Q, T_2, T_3 and

$$(A) \quad T_3 = T_k + (T_2 - T_k)e^{-\frac{kF}{Gc}}$$

$$(B) \quad Q = Gc(T_2 - T_3)$$

in which G expresses the weight of the gases flowing through each section of the flues per second, and c is the specific heat, of which the mean value is 0.25 for bituminous coal fuel.

The weight of a column of air of the external temperature T_0 and a height $h_0 + h_1$, representing the difference of pressure $p_0 - p_4$ per square meter, the point is to determine the height h above the level of the grate to which the gases can be raised in the atmosphere. This would be the height for the chimney.

In this calculation there should be taken into account; 1st, the diminution of atmospheric pressure due to the height h; 2d, the diminution of the

pressure of gas for the same height; 3d,
the mechanical work consumed by the
ascent of the gas through this height;
4th, the velocity of **the** escaping gas at
the top of the chimney. This outflow
cannot evidently take place unless the
pressure on the escaping gas is **at least**
equal to the atmospheric pressure.

In order to calculate the upward velocity of the gases in the chimney, **we**
make **use of** the equation

$$\frac{u\,du}{g} = -ds - \mathrm{RT}\frac{dp}{p} - \lambda\frac{ds}{d_m}\frac{u^2}{2g},$$

in which p is the pressure at the top of
the chimney and d_m is the mean diameter.

If we represent by u_1 T_1 and p_1 respectively, the velocity, the absolute
temperature and the pressure of the gas
at the base of the chimney; also by
u_a T_a and p, the same quantities at the
upper outlet of the chimney; the integra-
tion of the preceding equation, if we take
$T_m = \frac{1}{2}(T_1 + T_a)$ for the mean temperature of the chimney, also $u_m = \frac{1}{2}(u_1 + u_a)$
for the mean velocity, will give for the
term relating to the resistance of friction

$$\frac{u_a^2 - u_4^2}{2g} + \lambda \frac{h}{d_m} \frac{u_m^2}{2g} + h = RT_m \log\left(\frac{p_4}{p}\right).$$

On the other hand we shall have for the height h of a column of air, at the temperature T and under the upper and lower pressures of p_0 and p,

$$h = RT_2 \log\left(\frac{p_0}{p}\right).$$

Combining the preceding equations we get:

$$RT_0 \log\left(\frac{p_0}{p_4}\right) = h \frac{T_m - T_0}{T_m} - \frac{T_0}{T_m} \cdot$$
$$\left\{ \frac{u_a^2 - u_4^2}{2g} + \lambda \frac{h}{d_m} \cdot \frac{u_m^2}{2g} \right\}.$$

The first number of this being only the value of $h_0 + h_1$, the height of the chimney will be given by the formula:

$$(3) \quad h = (h_0 + h_4) \frac{T_m}{T_m - T_0} + \frac{u_a^2}{2g}$$
$$\left\{ 1 - \left(\frac{u_4}{u_a}\right)^2 + \lambda \frac{h}{d_m}\left(\frac{u_m}{u_a}\right)^2 \right\} \frac{T_0}{T_m - T_0}$$

in applying which to find approximate values of h, the following hypothesis is employed:

From the fundamental equation $pv = RT$, and from the equation $fu = G'v$ we deduce

$$u = G'R\frac{T}{pf},$$

G being the weight of gas in kilograms which passes each section of the chimney in a unit of time with the velocity u.

The influence of the change of pressure p upon the variation of the velocity u is so small that we may neglect it, while we have to regard the influence of change of temperature and of cross section, and we have with sufficient exactness:

$$\frac{u_{,}}{u_a} = \frac{T_{,}}{T}\frac{f_a}{f_{,}}$$

and

$$\frac{u_m}{u_a} = \tfrac{1}{2}\left(\frac{u_{,}}{u_a} + 1\right).$$

We can calculate from equation (3) a first approximate value of h, after having assigned proper values to f_a $f_{,}$ and f_m, also to T_a according to the value of $T_{,}$ and according to the material of which the chimney is built. It is necessary also to determine $\dfrac{u_{,}}{u_a}$ and $\dfrac{u_m}{u_a}$, since in the term $\dfrac{h}{d_m}$ we substitute the approximate value $(h_0 + h_1)\dfrac{T_m}{T_m - T_0}$.

From this value of h a more exact value of T_a can be deduced by employing the equation

$$T_a = T_0 + (T_4 - T_0)e^{-\dfrac{k_s\,F_s}{G_s\,c}}$$

in which k_s represents the coefficient of conductivity of heat for the sides of the chimney; F_s the area of the interior surface; G_s the weight of gas per hour passing any section of the chimney; $c = 0.25$, the specific heat of the gaseous mixture.

For chimneys of masonry, we take $K_s = 1.4$ to 2 according to the thickness of the sides. For chimneys in plate or sheet iron $k_s = 6$; $G_s = 22B_n$; B_n being the weight of coal consumed per hour on all the grates whose fires lead to the same chimney.

From this value of T_a we easily deduce more exact values of T_m, $\dfrac{u_4}{u_a}$ and of $\dfrac{u_m}{u_a}$.

We shall then be able to obtain a second approximate value of h, which may be regarded as a definite value.

We shall have for the magnitude of f_a the entrance to the chimney,

$$f_a = \frac{G_s u_a}{3600 \, u_a}$$

or $\qquad f_a = 0.062 \frac{T_a}{u_a} \cdot \frac{B_n}{3600}.$

In calculating $\frac{f_a}{f_{\text{\tiny 4}}}$ there are three cases to be considered:

1st. The transverse section of the chimney decreases from the bottom upwards; $f_a < f_{\text{\tiny 4}}$. (Fig. 1.)

2d. The transverse section is everywhere the same; then $f_a = f_{\text{\tiny 4}}$. (Fig. 2.)

3d. The section increases from below upwards; then $f_a > f_{\text{\tiny 4}}$. (Fig 3.)

When f_a is less than $f_{\text{\tiny 4}}$, the ratio varies from 0.40 to 0.64 for chimneys constructed either in masonry or iron according to height. We may take therefore as a mean value $\frac{f_a}{f_{\text{\tiny 4}}} = 0.52$.

The second condition of course gives

$$\frac{f_a}{f_4} = 1.$$

For the third case we take $\dfrac{f_a}{f_4} = 1.5.$

With regard to the temperatures T_4 and T_a we may introduce as first values in the calculation

$$\frac{T_4}{T_a} = 1.06 \text{ for chimneys in masonry.}$$

and $\dfrac{T_4}{T_a} = 1.10$ for iron chimneys.

For the velocity u_a with which the gas ought to escape from the chimney, we should take a rather large value for fear of interference by downward currents of air. The value of u_a should never be less than two meters.

Suppose that to calculate the dimensions of a masonry chimney, we admit that $\dfrac{T_4}{T_a} = 1.06$. We shall then obtain the following values:

For the first type, (Fig. 1)

$$\frac{u_4}{u_a} = 1.06 . 0.55 = 0.55 ; \qquad \frac{u_m}{u_a} = 0.775$$

thus $h = (h_0 + h_1) \dfrac{T_m}{T_m - T_0} + \dfrac{u^2 a}{2g}$

$\left\{ \lambda \dfrac{h}{d_m} \cdot 0.6 + 0.7 \right\} \dfrac{T_0}{T_m - T_0},$

for the second type, (**Fig. 2**)

$$\dfrac{u_4}{u_a} = 1.06 ; \quad \dfrac{u_m}{u_a} = 1.03$$

then $h = (h_0 + h_1) \dfrac{T_m}{T_m - T_0} + \dfrac{u^2 a}{2g}$

$\left\{ \lambda \dfrac{h}{d_m} \cdot 1.06 - 0.24 \right\} \dfrac{T_0}{T_m - T_0} ;$

for the third type, (Fig. 3)

$$\dfrac{u_4}{u_a} = 1.06 \cdot 1.5 = 1.59 ; \quad \dfrac{u_m}{u_a} = 1.3 ;$$

then $(h = h_0 + h_1) \dfrac{T_m}{T_m - T_0} + \dfrac{u^2 a}{2g}$

$\left\{ \lambda \dfrac{h}{d_m} \cdot 1.7 - 1.53 \right\} \dfrac{T_0}{T_m - T_0}.$

It is easy to see that for all forms the total height of the chimney depends; 1st, upon the amount of resistance encountered by the gases in the flues and through the fuel; 2d, upon the velocity of escape of the gases. The second term is very small compared with the first, and as the variation of h for one type or the other depends on the second term, it is evident that the employment of type No. 3 cannot lead to a notable diminution of the height which it is necessary to use in No. 1. On the contrary the height becomes even less for the chimney contracted in the upper part than for the cylindrical form or for that which enlarges upwards; if it is demanded that the velocity of escape of the gases u_a be the same for the three types, the reason is that for the first form the resistance due to friction is more feeble. The fact should not be lost that in consequence of the large value of u_4 for the 3d type compared with the value of the same function for the 1st type, that the specific pressure p_4 would be much less in the first case than in the second; consequently the enlargement of the chimney towards the top would occasion a stronger current of hot gases at the bottom.

If on the other hand we desire that the

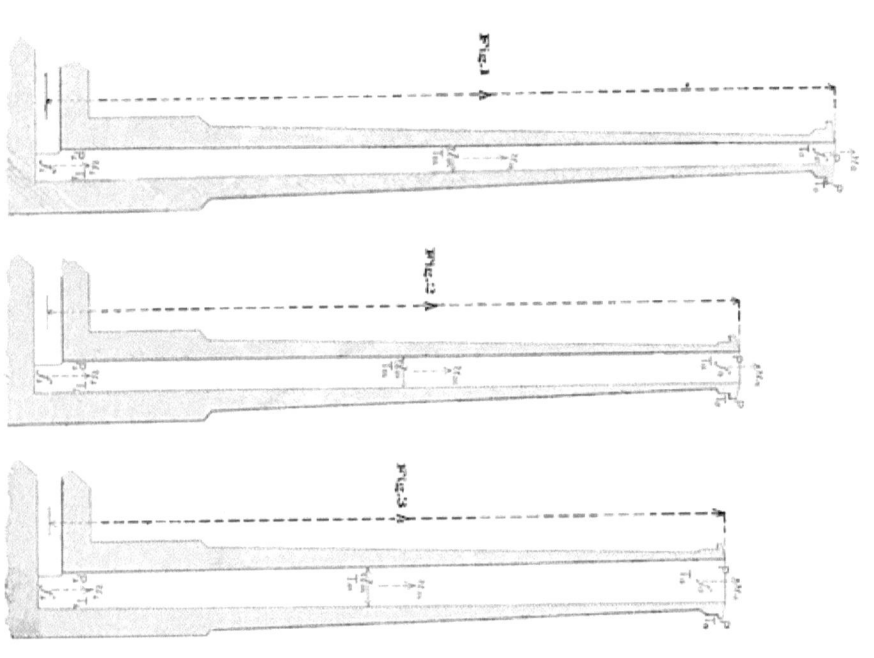

value of u_4 be the same for the three types, for equal ratios of temperatures and pressures, we shall have for the chimneys:

Fig. 1, $\qquad u_a = 1.82\, u_4,$

Fig. 2, $\qquad u_a = 0.94\, u_4,$

Fig. 3, $\qquad u_a = 0\ 63\, u_4.$

Let for example, for the

$\qquad$ 1st form $u_a = 4$ meters consequently $u_4 = 2^m.2.$

$\qquad$ Let in 2d form $u_a = 2^m.07$ and in $\qquad$ 3d form $u_a = 1^m.39$

With this feeble velocity of escape, the draft of the chimney would be easily reversed by the wind.

Take as an example a brick chimney designed to discharge the products of combustion from three boilers of equal size. Allowing for each boiler a heating surface of 60 square meters, and requiring a consumption of 100 kilos of coal per hour; the length of the flues being 30 meters, and their mean cross section $f = 0.2$ sq. meter; we have $d = \dfrac{4f}{F} = 0.^m25.$

Let $T_2 = 1300°$; $T_l = 420°$; $G = 2200^k$,

we shall have according to (A)

$$T_b = 420 + (1300 - 420)\, e^{-\frac{10.60}{2200.0,25}} = 520°\,;$$

and according to (B)

$$Q = 2200 \times 0.25(1300 - 520) = 429000^c.$$

(The heat directly radiated not being included.)

For $T_0 = 280°$ we shall have:

$$u_0 = \frac{G v}{3600 f} = \frac{2200 \times 0.8}{3600 \times 0.2} = 2^m.45$$

and according to equation (2):

$$h_1 = 0.306 \left\{ \frac{3 \times 1300 + 1 \times 520}{280} \right.$$

$$+ 0.08 \cdot \frac{30}{0.25} \left(\frac{429000}{20 \times 60 \times 280} + \frac{420}{280} \right.$$

$$\left. -2\, \frac{1300 - 520}{280} \right\} = 11^m.3.$$

Assuming $h_0 = 5^m.5$ we shall have:

$$h_0 + h_1 = 16^m.8.$$

Since the heated gases are cooled in passing through the horizontal conduit, we shall have to admit that t e absolute temperature T_1 is only 500° at the base of the chimney; whence

$$T_a = \frac{500}{1.06} = 470° \text{ and } T_m = \tfrac{1}{2}(500 + 470)$$
$$= 485°$$

We will take the velocity of escape of the gas, $u_a = 6$ meters, so that when only one boiler is used the velocity will be 2 meters; we then have:

$$u_a^2 = 1^m.835,$$

and equation (4) gives:

$$f_a = 0.062\frac{470}{6} \cdot \frac{300}{360} = 0.405 \text{ sq. meters,}$$

$d_a = 0.718$, or nearly 0.72 meters.

In order to provide, in case of need for a fourth boiler, we will take:

$$f_1 = 4f' = 4 \times 0.2 = 0.8 \text{ sq. meters.}$$

then $d_1 = 1.0$ meter, and

$$d_m = \tfrac{1}{2}(1.0 + 0.72) = 0.86 \text{ meters.}$$

We now have

$$\frac{u_1}{u_a} = \frac{500}{470}\frac{0.405}{0.800} = 0.54 \text{ and } \frac{u_m}{u_a} = 0.77.$$

The first approximate value then is

$$h = 16.8 \; \frac{485}{485-280} + 1.835$$

$$\left\{ 0.08 . 0.593 \; \frac{46}{0.86} + 0.708 \right\} \frac{280}{485-280}$$

$h = 39.665 + 8.133 = 47^m.798$, say **48 meters.**
We obtain **more** exactly

$$T_a = 280 + (500 - 280) \; e^{-\frac{1.6.130}{6600.0.25}} = 473°.$$

This result accords so well with the **value** $470°$ introduced above in the **calculations** of T_a, **that** it will not be necessary to make any **correction** in the **estimated** height of 48 meters.

We have $u_4 = 0.54 \times 6 = 3.24$ meters **for** the velocity **with** which the **gas** enters a chimney whose cross section diminishes upward. **(Fig. 1.)**

If a cylindrical chimney be used **(Fig. 2)** for which **the** velocity of escape $u_a = 0.94 \times 3.24 = 3.046$ meters, the **height** h will be reduced to :

$$h = 39.665 + 0.473$$

$$\left\{ 0.08 \; \frac{42}{1.0} \; 1.06 - 0.124 \right\} \frac{280}{485-280}$$

$h = 39.665 + 2.221 = 41^m.886$, or 42^m.

For a chimney, wider at the top than
the bottom, for which $\dfrac{f_a}{f_4} = 1.5$, we have

$u_a = 0.63 \cdot 3.24 = 2^m.04$ and

$h = 39.665 + 0.212$

$$\left\{ 0.08 \frac{41}{1.12}\ 1.7 - 1.53 \right\} \frac{280}{485 - 485}$$

$h = 39.665 + 0.999 = 40^m.664$, or 41^m.

The employment of the forms repre-
sented in figures 2 and 3 leads to a re-
duction in the estimated height of 6 or 7
meters, but the velocity of the escaping
gases is reduced from 6 to 2 or 3 meters,
which might lead to serious inconvenience
when only one boiler is at work instead of
three. In such a case a chimney of the
third type, the velocity of the escaping
gases would only be $\frac{2}{3}$ meter.

In order to diminish the downward
action of the wind, the chimney may be
surmounted by a conical cap. Many con-
structors do not approve of the widened
top, although it allows of greater width

to the orifice and therefore greater facili-
ties for changing the direction of the
currents of air at the summit of the
chimney.

www.ingramcontent.com/pod-product-compliance
Lightning Source LLC
Chambersburg PA
CBHW022342020726
47500CB00004B/1235